NAME .... Emily Price

ADDRESS .... Laurel Walk, London,
England, ~~Europi~~ European Union

DESTINATION .... San Francisco, USA

PHONE NUMBER 01702 431689

D1395146

Right now,
I'm not sure if...

I ♥ SF

London Theatre Weekly

'TORN ASUNDER' to tour **USA**

My

TOTALLY SECRET

Diary

On Stage in America

(with mostly awful actorish people, ~~espesh~~ especially the girls)

Belonging <u>entirely</u> to me,

Polly Price

So PLEASE KEEP OUT!

Dee Shulman

MY TOTALLY SECRET DIARY: ON STAGE IN AMERICA
A DOUBLEDAY BOOK 978 0 385 61492 4

First published in Great Britain by Doubleday,
an imprint of Random House Children's Books
A Random House Group Company

This edition published 2008

1 3 5 7 9 10 8 6 4 2

Text handwritten by Dee Shulman

RANDOM HOUSE CHILDREN'S BOOKS
61–63 Uxbridge Road, London W5 5SA

www.**kids**at**randomhouse**.co.uk
www.**rbooks**.co.uk

Addresses for companies within The Random House Group Limited can be
found at: www.randomhouse.co.uk/offices.htm

THE RANDOM HOUSE GROUP Limited Reg. No. 954009

A CIP catalogue record for this book is available from the British Library.

Printed and bound in Singapore

July 24th

Some kids have happy, carefree lives...

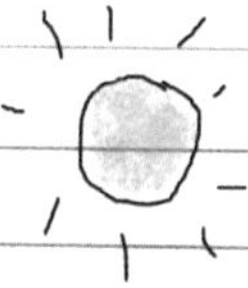

with NORMAL parents...
eating NORMAL food...

saying NORMAL things...

Did you have a nice day at school, dear?

Sadly I am not one of them. I am the **tragic** victim of a HOPELESS parent.

And I can think of only one way to deal with my misery, and that's to write it all down.

So this is my

DIARY of GLOOM

This was never meant to be my diary of gloom. It's not even a real diary. It's actually the SPECIAL OFFER notebook I bought yesterday with my holiday money.

I wasn't even going to start using it till I got to America and had some stuff to stick in it - like my plane ticket, postcards, maps and other important documents of my Journey.

SPACE RESERVED FOR IMPORTANT JOURNEY DOCUMENT No ①

← This was the only thing that fitted — TRULY DISGUSTING! ~~Cinomon~~ cinnamon gum - the WORST invention EVER

④

In actual fact this book was lying happily at the bottom of my suitcase, with a few other specially chosen items...

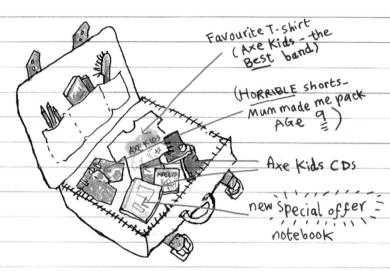

Favourite T-shirt (Axe Kids – the Best band)

(HORRIBLE shorts– Mum made me pack AGE 9)

Axe Kids CDs

new special offer notebook

...But desperation forced me to ~~misuse misapropreate~~ take it out and use it.

When I say <u>desperation</u> I am not exaggerating.

<u>I</u> had been packed and ready for <u>DAYS</u>.

<u>Mum</u>, on the other hand, hadn't.

The HOPELESS parent

Mum started packing when the taxi driver arrived.

By the time he
was onto his 3rd
cup of herbal tea –

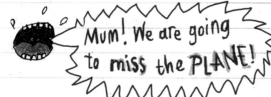

I HAD to take action.

Mum! We are going to miss the PLANE!

I just can't decide what to pack, Polly-dolly!
Should I take the PINK? Does the colour
really suit me? I love the blue linen but
it creases so badly... and the black,
which is so versatile, might look a bit...
well – black – in America...

In the end we compromised. She took everything.

And me and the taxi driver lugged it into the taxi.

I am now sitting in that very taxi, taking deep calming ~~breths~~ breaths and trying to keep my pen from tearing through the page of

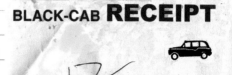

BLACK-CAB **RECEIPT**

AMOUNT £ 7.50

my lovely new notebook. Mum is sitting cross-legged next to the taxi driver, chanting *Deringa. gaw. gaw - Nicker. anga*

Don't bother looking those words up. Mum invented them. She is repeating them in a slow *droning* voice. They are supposed to keep her **centred**. They aren't ~~keeping~~ me ~~centered~~ centred though. <u>PLUS</u> the chanting is making it very difficult to ~~consent~~ concentrate on writing.

So I'm going to draw some pictures till she finally gets centred. shuts up

ME

<u>NAME</u> Polly - <u>not</u> a cool name, especially when
   your mother adapts it to Pollypop (or worse).
   But I will <u>never</u> reveal what Polly is short for
<u>AGE</u> Nearly 12
<u>JOB</u> Trying to keep S<u>ANE</u>

<u>MP3 PLAYER</u>
highly important
tool for shutting
out mothers

<u>PHONE</u>
even more
important
(though Mum's
said no one's
allowed to phone
me in America because
it costs her money)

NEW
NOTE BOOK
DIARY

<u>JEANS</u>
Mum hates
them

<u>TRAINERS</u>
Mum hates
them even
more than
Jeans

MUM

NAME Arabella Diamonte (I think she made it up herself)

AGE Thirty-something

JOB Actress
(need I say more?)

SHADES
Won't leave home without them

MAKE-UP
Way too much for a mother

HAIR - Too long and colourful for a person of her age

LONG RED FINGERNAILS
Her excuse for not being able to carry any luggage

CLOTHES
What can I say???

HEELS
How can you do anything in those?

At last! She's stopped chanting and is reapplying her make-up. This should give me loads of time to fill in some ~~relevant felt~~ relevant facts... like:

| WHERE WE ARE GOING | Answer: San Francisco!

| WHY | Answer: The play my mum's in...

TORN ASUNDER

...IS opening there, and I'm going too — if we ever make it onto the plane.

A WEEK AGO

excited
radiant
smiling

Looking at me now you'd never guess that I've been looking forward to this FOR WEEKS.

NOW

visible sweat
signs of ~~exhorst~~ exhaustion
~~stw~~ quivering wreck

Hey — We've arrived at the airport!!!

Gotta go!

ON THE PLANE

Because we were so late, Mum managed to persuade the staff all her luggage was

ESSENTIAL! My shoes are Vital! HATS - absolutely imperative—

OK, ok, get them on the plane!

We'd just squeezed past all the **PUNCTUAL** People into the last 2 seats... when Mum stood up.

I can't possibly sit in THIS SEAT! There's no room for my LEGS! I will only be comfortable in an AISLE seat!

The stewardess's *smile* had started to look distinctly like a snarl.

WOULD YOU KINDLY SIT DOWN, MADAM - WE ARE ABOUT TO TAKE OFF!

Mum refused to sit down. LOUDLY.

Everyone shuffled uncomfortably. Especially the long-legged man in the aisle seat next to me.

Trying to look engrossed in his magazine

We could all get on with the journey if *someone* would swap seats.

I knew she'd win.
It was just a matter of time.

23 seconds to be precise.

We exchanged looks of resigned misery.

Mum, on the other hand, was all happiness and joy.

> Isn't this exciting, Pollypops?
> I just **LOVE** travelling
> by air!

Happiness and joy at
Mum's level must be
tiring, because as soon as
we took off she fell asleep.

Mum must **NEVER** see this
(taken with my mobile)

This has given me the perfect peace and
quiet to catch up on the whole journey so far.

I think I've even got
time to add some
impressive ~~geo geogey~~
geography information.

According to the little
TV screen in front of me—

Uh-Oh! Mum's just stood up.
BAD SIGN.

Not even a
bit blurry!

Aghh!
She's waving!
DANIEL, DARLING! Is the whole cast on the plane? How marvellous!
She's clambering over passengers - I can't look!
WAIT— the head steward has stepped in...
MADAM - this is not - - My GOODNESS ... You're not A-A-Arabella-?
I am She!
regal voice
H-H-How utterly thrilling! Is there anything I can do for you?
BAD MOVE - stew-boy
Why, you SWEET man - there is one TINY thing you could do...
dazzling smile

The company and I would so LOVE to have a little party - perhaps in the First Class section - to cause less of a disturbance?

Mum looking around ~~compash compasson~~ compassionately

Well - ahem - absolutely! It's quite empty in there actually.

flattened

He's rewarded by one of Mum's suffocating hugs. But he seems truly happy, leading Mum and all the actors away.

I slide down in my seat. If I shut my eyes they may go without me...

BUM.

drag

15

LATER (that day/night)

↙ not quite sure

USEFUL TIP

If you close your eyes for long enough and turn your MP3 player up really loud you can actually block out your mother and her friends and even fall asleep.

But it takes a lot of hard ~~conson~~ concentration and it is NOT pleasant to be woken up again.

POLLY - WE'VE ARRIVED! WAKE UP! There's all my luggage to carry!

I looked at my watch ... nearly MIDNIGHT!

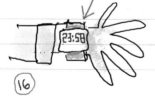

I looked out the window... Sunshine? →

16

never will my
true name be revealed

Really ~~[redacted]~~, Polly!
Has that dreadful Miss Pukeit
taught you nothing about
international time differences?
What does she do all day?

Actually –
Miss Pugitt

Now please stop
blinking inanely
at your watch – I'd
like to get to the
hotel before the
first performance.

Can't remember much
about the journey from
the airport – I must
have dozed off again.
But I am now in a

USA AIRLINES ✈
BOARDING PASS
NAME OF PASSENGER
PRICE/HYPPOLITAMISS

TO
LONDON HEATHROW
SAN FRANCISCO INT
USA AIRLINES

CARRIER FLIGHT ———— CLASS DATE ———— TIME
AA AATION **142** **O**

GATE   BOARDING TIME   SEAT   SMOKE
9   **745A**   **26A**   **NO**

ADDITIONAL SEAT INFORMATION
PCS   CK.WT.   UNCK.WT.   SEQ.NO.   CK.WT.
BAGGAGE ID NR.
COUPON AIRLINE   FORM SERIAL NO.   CK
45Q / SFO

**GROUP
5**

YET ANOTHER RELEVANT
DOCUMENT OF JOURNEY

SAN FRANCISCO HOTEL

sitting – well, lying, on a big comfy bed

(17)

July 25th   Next Morning ^{← or so they say}

Breakfast, Polly-poppet - come along!

She's just woken me up <u>AGAIN.</u>

? ? ?

What time-zit?
Where am I?

The truth is I've been dragged around by my mum
long enough not to let details like waking up in a
strange bed worry me.

I HAVE STRATEGIES

On this occasion I decided the best strategy was to
shut my eyes and go back to sleep.

I've just woken up again — STARVING... and my
brain is now working well enough to fix on one
important word - Breakfast

To find breakfast requires me to activate   ^{This has never failed me →}

<u>EMERGENCY STRATEGY   NO. 2 - The Nose</u>

18

THE NOSE in this case meant following the divine hotel breakfast smell ... down 2 flights of stairs into ~ YES...

THE DINING ROOM!!!

Mum would have been hard to miss.

I sat down opposite her.

Hi honey! How do you like your eggs? Sunnyside up, over-easy, two on a raft?

I thought Americans spoke English!

The best I could do in the ~~ce~~ circumstances was point at the plate Mum was tucking into, which was filled with...

waffles
fried potatoes
← eggs
← SAUSAGES???

Mum's eating **MEAT**??? She's supposed to be **VEGETARIAN!**
Actually she's supposed to be **VEGAN** ← the PUREST kind of vegetarian
At least she has been for the past 8 months - since she
entered her ~~BUDDIS~~ ~~BUDH~~ BUDDHIST Phase ←

So I'm sitting here watching Mum stuffing sausages
and **fried eggs** into her mouth...

also NOT Allowed!

...and I am **UTTERLY SPEECHLESS** →

PLONK!

WOW!
LOOK what's just
landed in front of me! →

MUM'S BUDDHIST PHASE - Total Nighmare! Mum turning
Vegan has meant **ME** giving up everything I love: sweets
chocolate, custard, ice cream, sausages, nuggets, treacle
pudding etc. Mum wouldn't even let me eat chips (which
I've recently found out Vegans are allowed) because she
believes ALL FRIED FOOD is POISON. So practically all we've
been allowed to eat for MONTHS is beans and rice.
And salad. I'm probably clinically ~~malnutish~~ starved.

I have just decided that UTTERLY SPEECHLESS outrage *is* important – but not *as* important as scoffing the lot before Mum turns Vegan again.

Uh-oh – She has just stood up.

Hurry up, darling – We're leaving for the theatre in 3 minutes.

Bup-Mum–

valuable chunks of waffle

Do try to enunciate, You can never hope for a career on the stage if you mumble–

As if!

I swallow hard.

But I thought we'd be looking round San Francisco and stuff—

said very clearly indeed

Don't be ridiculous! We have to *rehearse*! The **OPENING**'s in 3 days!

21

But the show's been on in London for a year – you must know it by now!

Raised eyebrow and withering look →

I give up! Good job this diary's secret.

Hyppolita – how many years have you been associated with me?

Is this how a normal mother talks?

Surely even a child of your limited observational skills will have noticed by now that every theatre is different? The staging has to be adapted. After all – we have to put on a glorious show for our American audience...

radiant smile for possible American audience in room →

And of course the **children** are still quite new to the play...

What children?

Heavens above, child, does your brain retain nothing? The -children-in-the-cast! This will be a marvellous opportunity for you to meet them.

Before I can come up with an ESCAPE strategy, I am being dragged out of the hotel and along the streets of San Francisco. It's not at all easy to catch up with your diary every time you stop at a crossing.

STARS AND STRIKES

Especially if you have a mother who keeps jogging you when she grabs your shoulder to cross the road

← IMPORTANT JOURNEY DOCUMENT
spotted on ground by traffic light!

THE THEATRE - A bit later

Things are not good.

My mum has just WOOSHED us through a bunch of actors, towards 2 whispering girls...

super straight hair

blonde highlights

tan - definitely not from normal playing in the garden

clothes with cool labels from shops normal people don't even know about

... girls who were instantly ~~recon~~ recognizable as CHILD ACTORS.

THEATRE KIDS

Most kids hanging around theatres are there because they <u>have no choice.</u> They are the <u>tragic</u> victims of show-off parents, who drag them around the place, forcing them to read old comics in total silence, <u>for hours</u> in pokey dressing rooms.

> I am obviously in this catergory

But then there's this other breed of kid:
THE CHILD ACTOR

He or she is there because she <u>wants</u> to be there. You can usually rely on the fact that THE CHILD ACTOR is the last child on earth who any <u>normal</u> person (me) would want to spend their summer in San Francisco hanging round with.

Back to the whispering girls...

> Ah! Here you are, girls—

The two blonde highlights looked absolutely ~~thrilled~~ at having their conversation interrupted.

26

... NIGEL - the Director →

Welcome, Welcome, Welcome!

no idea what this means →

Isn't this a FABULOUS beejoo of a theatre? And I know the show is going to be HUGE here - ticket sales are FANTASTIC - especially for the opening.

The actors are all spellbound, so I've managed to sneak away from the girls and found a ~~sectoo~~ secluded seat. From here I can check everyone out. Most eyes are gazing adoringly at Nigel, but I've just caught 2 ☉ ☉ staring straight back at me! Below the eyes is a mouth, which is grinning. ↗
It belongs to a face I haven't seen before - a boy, a couple of years older than me probably. But he looks <u>way</u> too normal (nice) to be one of the **actor kids**. So whose poor son can he be? I can't see anyone who looks much like him — <u>WAIT</u> - there's another boy, also blond, about the same age!
<u>THIS PLACE IS LITTERED WITH KIDS!</u>

Blah blah — darlings... drone blah drone

The second boy hasn't spotted me - he's totally ~~fokus focusse~~ concentrating on Ophelia and Aurora... They've just passed him a note.

 Now all 3 are collapsing with laughter.  SNORT

LUCKILY FOR THEM nobody has noticed because Nigel has just run out of drone so everyone is breaking for coffee - ~~exe~~ except the stage managers, who are getting stuff ready for the ~~feher~~ rehearsal.

Actually I'm quite looking forward to this rehearsal now - ok - I actually <u>can't wait</u> to see the BLONDE HIGHLIGHTS trying to act like REAL people!

<u>OH NO!</u>

Something red and dangerous is coming over —

Darling - the children aren't needed today - so our TREASURE of a ~~sha~~ chaperone, Donna, has agreed that after lessons, she will take you along with the other children into San Francisco! Aren't you lucky?

Would you describe being stuck all afternoon with Ophelia, Aurora and <u>D</u>onna as **lucky**? ⟶

I don't think so.

> Er-actually, Mum-I was looking forward to watching you rehearse.

← winning smile

This **had** to work...

> How touching, darling! But tomorrow's rehearsal will be much better to watch-and this trip will be <u>such</u> fun! Anyway, imagine how delighted Miss Pukeit will be with the extra work!

> WHAT? You can't mean **I** have to do lessons as well?

> All the children are, Polly-doodle. You don't want to fall behind now, do you?

> But it's the **Summer holiday!**

I'm whining into the air. She's gone.

29

LATER

Before I had a chance to call the American Child Abuse Agency, Donna hauled me into the sort of pokey room that theatres specialize in...

THE THEATRE GREEN ROOM

Don't ask me why it's called a green room. I've never seen one that was actually green.

Aurora took this photo with her instant camera- and THREW it away!! (I fished it out- recognizing an important document)

no window

Dank paper cup with remains of coffee in it. This one also has ~~floofes~~ bright red lipstick decorating the rim.

smell of stale cigarettes in spite of NO SMOKING sign

Apart from these unsavoury items, the room also contained Aurora and Ophelia... along with the 2 boys I'd spotted in the auditorium.

Aurora and Ophelia wasted no time in marking out their territory.

lipsticky cup has had to settle for the floor.

Donna chose herself the least stained chair, folded herself into it, and picked up a magazine.

> OK, guys — an hour of school stuff and then we can go shopping... deal?

Aurora and Ophelia groaned.

The boy who'd been passing notes sat down by the girls and got a book out. He didn't open it though. He just whispered something to them, and they all started <u>vibrat</u>ing with laughter.

The other boy cleared his throat.

Hi, I'm Will.

He's **way** better looking than this (I've rubbed this drawing out about **20** times)

I liked him.
What was he doing here?

And that's Felix— we're sharing the role of Hugo in the play. Have you met the girls?

I was just about to answer, but Ophelia got there first.

Pollypop's mummy introduced us!

This apparently was **really** funny.

Pollypops!

Mummy!

Ha! Ha!

Will ignored them.

Do you need anything? Paper, pen?

Er...it's ok I've got my –

I just stopped myself in time. If I'd said DIARY in here, I'd be **dead**.

We sat down at a ropey old table. He got out a couple of books and started to read. I opened my diary really carefully so no one could see inside, and I've managed to catch up on today's events ~~extree~~ extremely ~~efish~~ efficiently.

wills Will William will Will Will WILL

I like the name **WILL**. I hope it's short for William William william

BUM! What was I thinking??? Now I have to buy some white correction stuff IMMEDIATELY.

Hey – looks like we're on the move. Donna has just put down her magazine and stood up.

LATER

We all trooped out into brilliant sunshine.

Will gave me an ~~exhasp~~ exasperated look, and I tried not to laugh.

PHEW! Comic strips take totally **AGES** to do!

35

Luckily for those of us who don't like stupid arguments (ME), Ron arrived, and put his arm round Donna, causing Ophelia and Aurora to:

① Shut up
  (a very good result)

dumbfounded

... then

② whisper
(not so good but still less annoying than arguing.)

Blissfully unaware, Ron and Donna set off towards the shopping mall with the rest of us trailing behind.

The mall was MASSIVE!!!

I would have taken a <u>million</u> photos if I hadn't left my mobile back at the hotel. Anyway I was so busy staring that it took me a while to notice Aurora's growing whine...

I'M STARVINGGG!

Huh! Starving but totally picky...

Euch! I'm not eating there!

—or there!

Eventually EVERYONE was starving.

—or there!

The diner that passed the Princess Aurora test was on the 5th floor (nothing suitable on floors 1-4). But I have to admit this one _was_ utterly DAZZLING!

shiny milkshake machine I think

incredibly shiny ~~crome~~ chrome

shiny

I hoisted myself happily up onto this stool.

Donna pulled me off it.

We're sitting at the tables.

Donna and Ron sat opposite each other kissing a lot.

Ophelia and Aurora sat next to each other giggling a lot.

cute bear!
YET ANOTHER
IMPORTANT
JOURNEY
DOCUMENT

Felix and Will sat by me, eating <u>a lot</u>

— and they'd just started telling some really good jokes... when

the <u>bill</u> came. Donna examined it, then told us that we each owed $9.

OK — I never wrote about the moment when my mum gave me a ~~wod~~ wad of money, and said, "Have a great time, darling."

I never wrote about it for a very good reason.
<u>It didn't happen.</u>
I had no money at all.

I wiggled my fingers around my jeans pockets anyway,
hoping for a miracle, while everyone else passed
bundles of dollars across to Donna.

Surely there was enough?
It looked like loads.
She counted the money.
Then she re-counted it.

> Someone hasn't paid.

For some reason, all eyes turned to me.

> Er-um-I'm sorry -I don't -er- have any...

> When they talk about America being THE LAND OF THE FREE they don't mean the _food_!

HA!

Obviously everyone found this hilarious ...!

well nearly everyone.

HA! HA! HA! HA! HA!

> It's OK, I've got enough to pay for Polly's. Come on, let's get out of here.

♥Will♥

> I'll pay you back...   ← croaked whisper

> Hey, you can get mine next time.

my hero

Aurora and Ophelia were in **Princess Heaven!**

In Orlando's nearly everything sparkled—including the 2 assistants—whose lip gloss shimmered into action whenever Ophelia or Aurora picked anything up.

Oh my! I just know that's going to look _fabulous_ on you! Are you looking for a special occasion?

We're going to need something really _spectacular_ for our **Opening Night**.

Totally ~~glamer glamour~~ divine.

Are _you_ in the show too, honey?

Eyelash extensions suddenly widened in my direction

Er-no...

Uhuh. So what are you then?

Who asks questions like this? No prizes for guessing who answers though...

She's _nothing_ — just here with her **mummy** — SNORT!

The lashes turned quickly back to the stars.

You girls <u>have</u> to try these on in our Regency ~~Sweet~~ Suite - it's Zelda Rose's favourite dressing room!

Have <u>you</u> got anything to try on, Missy?

lip gloss suddenly beamed towards <u>me</u>

Er- no, it's OK.

Ha! You don't have to p<u>a</u>y to try things on, you know, Polly-*poop*!

SNIGGER

Oh - get lost!

muttered not quite under my breath

Aurora snorted, and flounced off with Ophelia to the changing room, leaving me free to explore. And I have to admit the clothes were <u>AMAZING</u>.
<u>So</u> amazing, that it was only when I noticed the assistants closing the doors that I looked at my watch...

dropped off one of the dresses Ophelia took to try on

5:30

Oh no! We were supposed to meet back at the diner ½ an hour ago! I dashed to the changing rooms —

Ophelia, Aurora — we're late!

B-b-but they can't have done. We were together.

I rode down 3 escalators...

...Then up 2...

...and I was just contemplating PANIC...

...when I smelt the familiar whiff of...

I ran wildly towards the escalators, trying to work out which floor _I_ was on, and which floor the _diner_ was on. Neither answer came into my head.

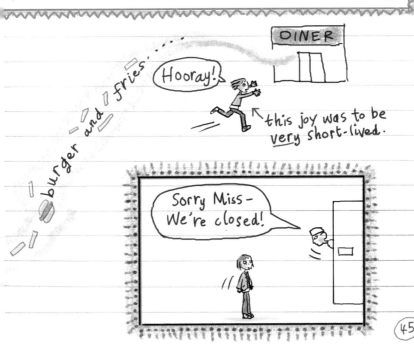

burger and fries...

Hooray!

DINER

← this joy was to be _very_ short-lived.

Sorry Miss— We're closed!

It took no time at all to come to a full assessment of the situation...

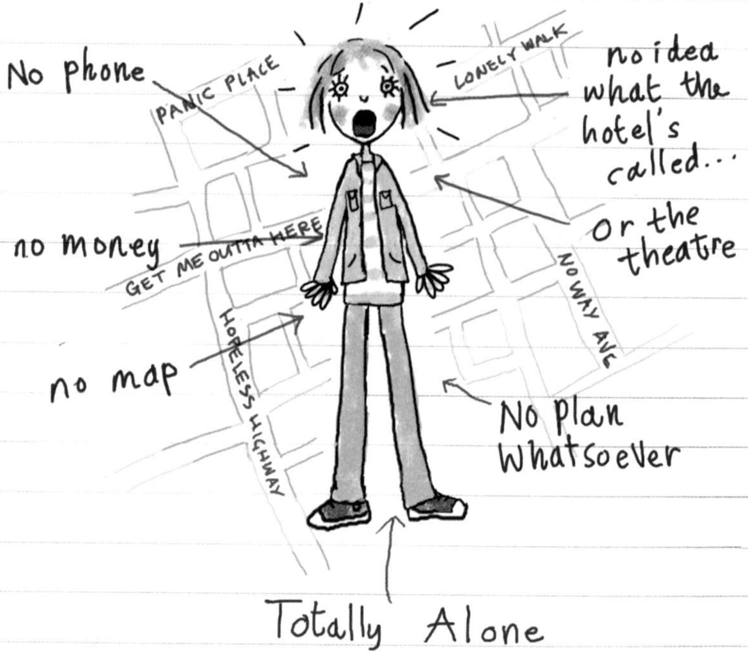

Totally Alone

I leaned against the diner window and shut my eyes, which you'd think would prevent tears from getting out, but they somehow found gaps and squished their way through. My only ~~consel~~ consolation was there was no one there to notice...

CORRECTION...

Polly?

Will?

sobby whisper

He handed me a tissue.

Where are the others?

Gone back to the theatre.

Without me?

mouth hanging attractively open

Aurora and Ophelia insisted you'd got bored and left... they were looking a bit shifty - so I sneaked back, just in case.

Thank you so much...

WILL

Hey, forget it - I've been looking out for my kid sister so long it's become a habit.

POP

By the time we got back to the theatre it was getting late –

but then I heard that familiar voice echoing round the auditorium –

YOU DID WHAT?

Phew! They were still rehearsing – I hadn't been missed – BIG Relief as my mum has a slight tendency to get hysteric –

ARE YOU TELLING ME THAT YOU LEFT MY CHILD ALONE – IN THE MIDDLE OF THIS CRIME-INFESTED CITY? gasp – SOMEONE TELL ME I DIDN'T ENTRUST MY DAUGHTER's LIFE TO THIS MORONIC LITTLE HALF-WIT! HAS ANYONE CALLED THE POLICE, THE ARMY, THE FIRE BRIGADE?

One look at Will's horrified expression confirmed my deepest fear... These weren't lines from the script.

Come on then, Poll, we'd better put her out of her misery.

Of course that could'nt be the end of it, could it?

After the ~~compubser~~ compulsory ~~sufer~~ suffocating sobby, soaking hug, there had to be this
MASSIVE ~~NEW~~ INQUISITION.

Mum wasn't interested in the FACTUAL version of events (mine or Will's).

She wanted BLOOD ← DONNA'S

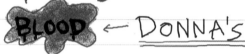

Nigel - there is No way we can entrust the PRICELESS lives of our young into the hands of that Feckless Fashion Failure!

Arabella, darling - we can't simply get rid of someone. There are all sorts of issues... and to be fair, legally - Donna's - ahem - responsibilities begin and end with the -er - child performers.

Bad tactical decision, Nigel...

Are you telling me that _MY_ child's life is worth _less_ than those precoshuss little princesses in the cast?

must look up this spelling

N-no - of course not, my love.

Indeed - I now wonder if perhaps I too am worth less than they are? Perhaps you will find the show a whole lot easier _legally_ to manage without Arabella Diamonte in the starring role? (heartrending) **SOB!**

Arabella-darling...

big actory hug

You know the show utterly depends on your marvellous ~~paw~~ portrayal...

look of adulation

I just think we are all a bit tired and overwrought...

soothing but firm

And we should discuss this again after a good night's sleep.

My mother was not soothed.

Come on, Hyppolita. We're leaving!

Forgot to bring diary down - so got this from reception!!!

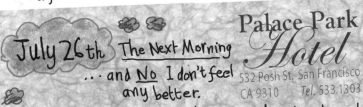

July 26th   The Next Morning

... and **No** I don't feel any better.

Palace Park Hotel
532 Posh St. San Francisco
CA 9310   Tel. 533.1303

Hunger has driven me down for breakfast, and I've been ~~lerk~~ lurking by the door, checking who's in there.

| THE GOOD NEWS | No sign of the girls - or Donna.

| THE BAD NEWS | Mum's in there... with Nigel.

So I'm going to have to skulk around out here till she - **BUM** - she's waving...

> Hyppolita, darling - over here! You simply **must** try the pancakes - they're miraculous!

They **must** be to have caused this transformation.

LAST NIGHT

Thunderous

THIS MORNING

Joyous

53

Then my plateful of pancakes arrives...

4 pancakes! swimming in maple syrup

blueberries

whip whipped cream

strawberries

And I begin to understand. In fact the pancakes almost completely distract me from the conversation.

Almost.

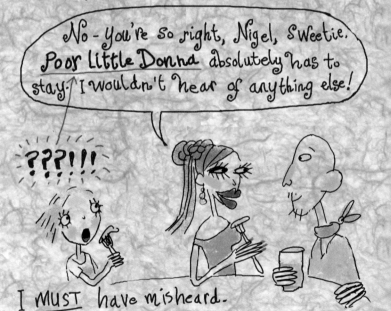

No - You're so right, Nigel, sweetie. _Poor little Donna_ absolutely has to stay. I wouldn't hear of anything else!

???!!!

I _MUST_ have misheard.

I see now that Polly was absolutely fine – probably wandered off in a world of her own. What a ~~garstly~~ ~~ghars~~ ghastly shock for **Poor Sweet Donna!** Do you know what, Nigel? I'm going to send Donna some flowers. Lilies would be perfect...

My mother is clearly having some sort of breakdown! Better take action.

Mum, can you hear me? Shall·I·call·a·doctor?

Polly - will you stop making an exibition of yourself and **sit down!** What is the matter with you?

Now that sounds more like my mother. I sit down, eyeing her ~~corshus~~ cautiously. Nigel breaks the silence.

Isn't your mother a wonderfully forgiving person, Polly? I knew that her warm and generous spirit would overcome all last night's ~~angwish~~ anguish...

Warm and generous spirit? Forgiving? **My mother??!** I am confused.

And it's so wonderful to be able to offer such a kindness to the adored niece of Letitia Milton!

Letitia Milton? Who's she?

utterly blank

You know, darling – the incredibly famous and powerful Letitia Milton!

← even more utterly blank

Honestly, Hyppolita – I sometimes wonder if you weren't accidentally swapped with some stupid woman's baby in the hospital...

Letitia Milton – Donna's aunt – is <u>the</u> Hollywood theatre critic! And she's asked for tickets to our Opening Night! Have you any idea what a review from Letitia Milton could mean?

faraway look →

Anyway, I'd better get off and order those lilies. Buck up, Polly–Dolly. We'll be leaving for the theatre in ten minutes.

Palace Park Hotel
532 Posh St. San Francisco CA 93410 (415) 533.1303

How am I supposed to grow up <u>NORMAL</u>??

57

AN HOUR LATER

I am sitting in a dark auditorium in a dark dark mood - waiting for the rehearsal to start.

Luckily I've managed to slip into my seat more or less unnoticed.

BUT HOW LONG CAN I KEEP THIS UP ???

avoiding Donna, the princesses, and my warm forgiving mother?

At <u>Last</u> - the curtain's opening...

ABOUT 2 HOURS LATER (12.30 pm)

Wow! I've already seen Torn Asunder about a million times, and I know it ~~practicly~~ almost off-by-heart because I've spent hours testing Mum on her lines - but that was really good!!!

The weirdest thing is, I'm finding it really hard to hate Ophelia now, because on stage she was completely different... sort of lost and fragile.

OPHELIA
(as Sarah)

← wig - no sign of a highlight

horrible ragged dress

58

Daniel Hopkins played a ~~grotesk~~ ~~grotesck~~ grotesque prison-camp officer— with <u>no</u> consideration for human life... (especially Ron's)

DANIEL HOPKINS
(Prison-camp Officer)

evil expression

very realistic gun (which I can't draw)

Will played Ophelia's brother, who heroically managed to get them both out of the clutches of the evil Daniel Hopkins and find their mother. (guess who?)↗

Will was <u>BRILLIANT!</u>

I just have to go and congratulate ~~him~~ everyone.

WILL
(Hugo)

he must be <u>so</u> strong!

← wig (looked totally real!)

A BIT LATER

I rushed up the corridor and opened the first dressing-room door. __BAD MOVE__.

DRESSING ROOM 8

What are you doing here? Come to get someone else in trouble, have you?

Aurora snorting with laughter

Ha Ha Ha

me - just standing there - willing a clever, yet withering answer out of my mouth

I had to settle for a strangulated gurgle, but just about managed to turn round and walk out.

I got halfway down the corridor when I heard footsteps behind me. I was _not_ going to turn round.

Polly - slow down!

That was not Ophelia's voice.

Will?

I take it you didn't think much of the run-through?

Er - no - Will, _no_! I mean - y_es_ - I - it - was - er...

What was the matter with my mouth today? The best it could manage was -

Er.. you... it - was er... great...

Fortunately Will didn't seem to notice I'd lost the power of speech.

Now that he's gone I have to admit there
are <u>one</u> or <u>two</u> things I don't like:

<u>Olives</u> ◐ ◐ ◐ ← how could anyone eat these?

<u>goat's cheese</u> ← too smelly to put on a
plate – let alone in a mouth

<u>fishpaste</u>   yuk

<u>fish pie</u>   yuk

<u>fish curry</u>   yuk

<u>fish burgers</u>   OK ... anything with fish in it

<u>coleslaw</u> ← who came up with such a stupid idea?

<u>bananas</u> when they've been in your school bag
for 10 minutes. ↘

<u>pickled onions</u> 😣 YUK!

<u>Cabbage</u> ← EUCH!

<u>bread with bits in</u> ⇉

<u>meat with lumps in</u> ⇉

<u>capers</u> ○○○○○○○ ← who invented these?

<u>Mushrooms</u> 🍄 like eating slugs →

~~avere~~ <u>avocado pear</u> like eating slugs →

<u>AGGHH!!!</u> what'll I do when Will
comes back with something I can't eat?

LATER

The Good News

The brown paper bag that Will handed me...

genuine preserved ~~peace~~ piece of paper bag

contained an

EGG ~~BAY BAGUL~~ BAGEL

not a single mushroom or pickled onion to be seen!

The Bad News

I was just sitting in heavenly happiness next to Will, biting joyfully into my egg bagel, when...

Darling — I've been looking for you EVERYWHERE! I thought I'd find you with those charming girls Azalea and Oregano.

Her mouth suddenly snapped shut as she stood staring down at us.

During the silent lull, my heart sank. I just knew she was about to say something utterly ~~hidius~~ ~~hidious~~ hideous — like...

Has Pollypops got a little crush on you, Will?

or...

Hyppolita — I forbid you to sit with boys until you are twenty-one!

What she actually said was:

POLLY! You're eating WHITE bread! After all I've taught you about the benefits of the <u>whole</u> grain! Warren — a whole grain means a happy bowel—

I HAD to stop her.

MUM!

Er... I - er - really enjoyed the rehearsal this morning.

desperate change of subject →

Really, darling? But the lights went out during the tender love scene.

SUCCESS!

Well it looked great to me - so how good will it be when the lights are working?

Oh Polly - you ARE precious!

BIG LIPSTICKY HUG!

Are you watching this afternoon's rehearsal?

Probably. Did I have a choice?

Oh Polly-doodle — I am **so** pleased you're taking such an interest. Perhaps there is a <u>Thespian</u> deeply buried in that unexpected frame! See you later, darling — Walter, you'd better get yourself changed, we're starting at two.

I think this is Mum-speak for actory person — so obviously I pray there <u>isn't</u> one buried deep in my unexpected frame!

I'm only needed for a couple of scenes — do you want to come and hang out in the Green Room?

I was torn —

Should I go with Will (and maybe face the girls)?		<u>OR</u> Stay here alone?

Who was I kidding?

THE GREEN ROOM

Aurora in the Wig ↓

> What have you brought _her_ in for, Will? She'll just clutter up the place...

Luckily about 3 seconds later Felix and Aurora had to go on stage – leaving me, Will, Donna and Ophelia ~~rummage~~ rummaging through yesterday's bags of new clothes.

> What do you think, Will? I simply couldn't decide between these two so I got both! The woman in the shop couldn't believe I was only thirteen! She said I looked totally elegant! I do have quite a mature figure, don't I, Will? Which one do you think, Will? The red taffeta or the ~~terkw~~ turquoise silk?

> Shouldn't you have waited till you knew whether you or Aurora was doing the Opening, before splashing out on those outfits?

Will lent me this as I left my notebook in the auditorium

Oh - my agent says Nigel's crazy about my portrayal - so I'm pretty confident! Don't tell Aurora - she'd be devastated. Anyway we've all been invited to The Opening party whether we performed or not - so I need to stand out. I persuaded Aurora to buy the green velvet. She had wanted the red taffeta too, but it made her look fat so I had to tell her - as any true friend would.

Aurora - er Hi!

They want you on stage. Ophelia - To do the tunnel scene again...

But I did it this morning.

Nigel's trying something different - don't ask me what! That director's totally useless! He said he wanted me to be QUIETLY HYSTERICAL! I told him no one could be expected to act hysterical quietly. Instead of apologizing he told me to fetch you to have a go instead!
Oh, you've been trying on your new clothes...

Oops! It's really thin paper

They want me on stage right now?

In Costume?

Oh excuse my underwear, Will! No time for modesty!

Aurora stared ominously at the discarded red taffeta on the floor...

I thought I looked much better in that dress than Ophelia - but she wanted it so much I had to let her get it.

She picked it up and held it against herself.

Don't you think it suits my colouring much better than hers, Will? Shall I put it on for you? All right.

To be honest she looked OK - not fat at all - and I might have even told her, if she'd asked my opinion.

But she wasn't interested in what I thought.

Well, Will? How do I look? My dancing teacher says I have the grace of an angel.

She did her best to demonstrate this.
I did my best to keep a straight face.

I wish we could dance in the play. I suppose it's too tragic for dancing...

But you'd think there'd be an opportunity to sing, wouldn't you? Singing is my first love.

no idea how to spell this name

My voice teacher Giseppy Jigliany (yes the Gisseppi Jigglyani) told my mother that I could be truly sensational!

I'll sing you one of my favourites, shall I?

She didn't wait for an answer.

Darknesssss
Oh where is the moonlight?
Guide me far
From this black night
And take me awayyyy

The ~~fist~~ recital went on and on, each verse more warbly than the last - so by the time she finished, my head was throbbing.

That was - er - um - extraordinary, Aurora!

Oh thank you, Will! But I think I sing the dying love song from 'Angels' even better.

I can imagine, Aurora - but maybe you should rest your voice? We're opening the day after tomorrow.

Oh - singing's good for my voice - it needs lots of exercise. I'd better run through the high notes first...

Eeeeeeooooo—

AURORA!!!! What are you doing in my dress?

For one moment I actually felt sorry for Aurora — I needn't have.

Really, Ophelia — the red taffeta should be my dress. I tried it on first. And Will thinks I look better in it than you — don't you, Will?

Will blinking in shock.

Will, how could you? Just get that dress off right now, Aurora — or I'll never speak to you again.

Then Ophelia suddenly turned to me.

just sitting there
minding my own
~~big~~ business
(writing this
diary, in
fact)

And you can
wipe that look off
your face — I bet
you told her to
put the dress on,
didn't you?

AS IF!

Don't be ridiculous, Ophelia!

And I don't know why you're
still here, Will— Nigel wanted
you on stage five minutes ago!

But nobody told me!

I'm telling you now.

Will sped off, with me a milli-second behind him
— no way was I staying in there without him.
So I've spent the rest of the afternoon hiding
in the auditorium, watching bits of rehearsal, and
catching up on writing this whenever the lights
are bright enough - which has not been <u>at all</u> easy.

Nigel has just clapped his hands and called the cast together.

Marvellous, darlings – great day's work. First thing tomorrow morning I shall put up the final cast list. Obviously this is a matter of particular excitement for our younger cast members ...

Excitement? Er – understatement, Nigel!

And I know that you are all far too level-headed to feel serious disappointment...

What planet is he on?

The selection has nothing to to do with talent ...

Yeah-right!

Any of the four of you would do a fabulous job!

Big ~~insineer~~ insincere grin

Immediately after that we'll have our final dress rehearsal – followed by a BEACH PARTY! Donna, Rod and Daniel have kindly agreed to organize food and games – so all the rest of us have to do is find our cozzies and turn up!

JULY 27th Next Morning

Only an insane person would choose to be around the theatre when that cast list goes up, and I am <u>NOT</u> insane.

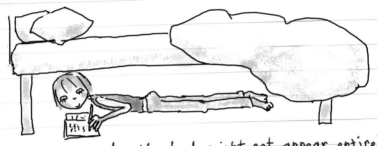

OK, hiding under the bed might not appear entirely sane - but I have to avoid detection... <u>UH-OH!</u>

HYPPO-DARLING?

<u>CLOSE ONE</u> ... but I think she's gone—

Hyppolita - you'll <u>ruin</u> your eyesight writing in ~~insufish~~ insufficient light— now come along or we'll be late.

Call the police! They're KILLING each other!

Donna, sweetie, calm down— you're sounding hysterical. Now— who is it you think might be killing each other?

Duh!

Luckily the girls weren't actually killing each other - because Will and Felix were heroically preventing them.

79

Oh shut up, Aurora — we've all heard what your dancing teacher told your mother ... it's not my fault the director ~~rekog~~ recognizes the genuine star. I don't see why you're taking it out on me... Is Felix attacking Will? <u>No</u> — he totally accepts that Will is the better actor for the role... And look what you've done to my arm! I'm going to phone my mother (sob) and my agent (sniff) ...

Pretty masterful actually, but keeping Aurora and Ophelia apart for the whole morning has not put a lid on this situation in my opinion. I mean — if someone spread a sheet of cling-film over Mt. Vesuvius would anyone feel safe?   <u>I DON'T THINK SO!</u> Especially if you lived in <u>Pompeii</u>

↑

quite impressive proof that I listened in at least 1 history lesson.

ON OUR WAY TO THE BEACH PARTY

It is with _no_ pleasure that I have to report
I was right. The volcano has _not_ been snuffed out.

> I'm beginning to slightly regret
> ever starting on this volcano thing.

Ophelia and Aurora clapped eyes on each other as
soon as we got onto the coach, and immediately
started to...

=HOWL=

in _horrific_ harmony.

And they could not be distracted.

What do you
call a man with
a seagull on his
head? **CLIFF**!
Ha ha!

Oh I do like to be
♪ Beside the seaside—

SCREECH

MOAN

I'm going to Sue
if I don't get some
peace!

I don't believe it – WE'RE STOPPING! The doors are opening! Got to get out before my head explodes!

USEFUL OBSERVATION

Any horrific noise coming from the mouths of ~~elinicty~~ clinically insane girls will drift painlessly away on the breeze, if you can get them off a coach and onto a beach.

It's a beautiful afternoon with a clear blue sky. Felix, Will and I have been helping Donna, Ron and Daniel lay out the rugs and food.

Got to stop writing to take some pics with my phone – Felix and Will are trying to get seagulls to fetch sticks!

Will's given up! ↓

seagull totally ignoring Felix

THE PICNIC (on the beach)

AHH! HELP!

Sweetie – if you're so worried about the noise, the heat and the mosquitos, why don't you go and sit in the coach? You could take your sandwiches.

What? In the coach? On my own? Are you joking? Unless...

Will – you've probably got sensitive skin. You should definitely come back to the coach with me... Will... Will?

It's ok, Ophelia – I'm fine here, thanks.

For one ~~FRESH~~ PRECIOUS, GLORIOUS moment, Ophelia was lost for words.

But things weren't quiet for long...

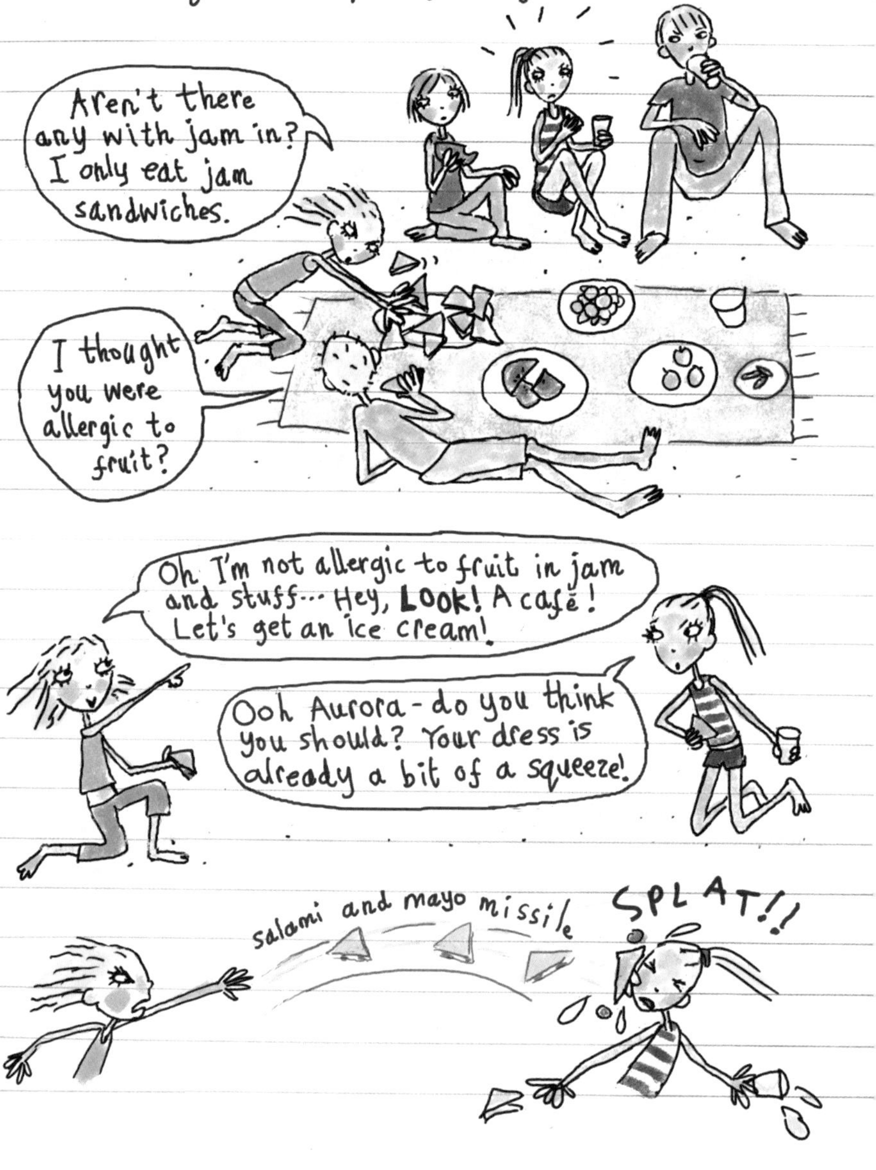

Aurora just turned her back on everyone, and Ophelia made a dash for the sea.

Then Daniel Hopkins (who I discovered is actually <u>not at all</u> like a prison-camp officer) tried to perk the party up by dancing around the rugs, showering us with handfuls of...

...chocolate bars →

and sweets

genuine bits of sweet wrapper

It was all going pretty well until it was Aurora's turn to count. She got to 100, opened her eyes, shuffled around for a couple of minutes, and then suddenly started to scream...

No, officially I should go with Will. After all, we're doing the Opening togeth—

Any more arguments and I eat the rabbit!

SILENCE.

Right — these are the rules...

I sat back down and have had a <u>nearly</u> peaceful time catching up on my diary.

apart from annoying comments from people like Ron.

Hope you're not working undercover for the gossip papers, Polly! We <u>would</u> be in trouble!

Of course, in between writing and ignoring Ron, I've been keeping an eye on the Treasure hunt.

Will and Aurora ↓

The 2 teams are on
different sets of clues
— so it's hard to tell
who's winning...

...but Felix and Ophelia
look a bit stuck... →

<u>Uh-Oh!</u> Ophelia's
shouting at Daniel:

It's not **FAIR!** You purposely gave the
others easier clues! And I got landed with
Felix, who can't work anything out. I've
had enough of this — I'm joining their team.

I <u>don't</u> believe it — she
<u>is</u> a<u>ctually</u> running off
to join the others...
leaving Felix
<u>SPEECHLESS!</u>

93

Will and Aurora are right on the other side of the beach... Ophelia has nearly reached them.
NO... she's not running any more ... she's ...

FLYING through ... the air ...

THWUNK!

That is the sound of her landing...

followed immediately by a blood-~~cerd~~ curdling...

SCREAM!

Everyone's running now — including me

<u>LATER</u> (on the Coach back to the hotel)

It's been <u>so</u> dramatic I haven't had a chance to write anything till now! So - where was I? Oh yes- Ophelia on the sand, covered in seaweed, wailing. Nigel was first on the scene.

OK- my love, where does it hurt?

Judging by the size and colour of her nose - quite a stupid question

Ab I bleeding?

No, Sweetheart - but you've got some good bruises! Do you think you can walk?

AGGHHH! My ANKLE! It's **agony!** I think it must be b-b-broken!

OK - not to worry! Ron, Daniel - can you carry our casualty to the road, while I hail a cab? Ophelia - we'll have you x-rayed and patched up in a flash!

As Daniel and Ron carried Ophelia back up the beach, she suddenly spotted the chocolate rabbit.

But, Will, it's not fair if I go off to hospital now, because...you'll -sob- win the rabbit -and I was just about to join your t-team.

Will's mouth dropping open

Fine, Ophelia— take the rabbit...

And he strode over, picked it up and handed it to her.

Will! The rabbit's not _yours_ to give! We were a _team_, you know! Why should _SHE_ get it?

But Ophelia kept an iron grip on the rabbit all the way to the taxi...

How could·sob· Aurora begrudge the rabbit to a person in as much pain as me?

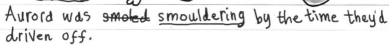

Aurora was ~~smoled~~ smouldering by the time they'd driven off.

Nobody around here considers _my_ feelings. It's always Ophelia, Ophelia, Ophelia. First she gets my role, then she gets MY chocolate rabbit! And I was _so_ looking forward to it. Chocolate is very good for ~~depresh~~ depression—but nobody here would notice how deeply depressed I've been all day - because all they care about is Ophel—

Aurora!!! Why don't you just GROW UP?

Aurora's mouth snapped shut. The rest of us stared in ~~ored~~ awed silence.

Ron broke the spell.

Hey! I know a really good beach game—

This went down really well...

Nooo! I don't want to play any more STUPID games. I hate it here. I want to go hoooome! I want my daddy! H-H-He'd buy me all the chocolate I could eat. And he'd let me wear the red dress for the Opening and he wouldn't make me play silly games, or stay with horrible people... I want my daaddy! I want to go hoome!

For Heaven's sake - she's bringing on a migraine!

For the first time ever Mum was NOT exaggerating. The volume was UNBEARABLE. So everyone agreed that enough was enough— it was definat definitely time to leave.

BACK AT THE HOTEL

As soon as we got back here - most
of the company (the <u>adults</u> basically)
vanished.

DADDY!

I'm off to lie down.

VROOM

Unfortunately Aurora didn't. She stomped
over to a corner of reception, and plonked
herself down. Donna was with Ophelia
at the hospital, so we couldn't just
leave Aurora - could we?

I want to go home!

In the end Felix
got some Cokes, and
we sat near her -
hoping someone
would finally come
and release us.

At last the revolving doors revolved Nigel, Donna and Ophelia into reception. Even from where I

was sitting I could see that Ophelia was _not_ having _a good face day._

Donna quickly disappeared with Ophelia into the lift, and Nigel came over to talk to us.

Well—there's nothing broken, thank the Lord! But she landed on her nose, which is, er—a little swollen... and unfortunately her ankle has got a rather nasty sprain... So she can't put any weight on it. She's getting the hang of the crutches pretty well though.

There was a moment's silence while we took this all in. Then Felix asked the question we'd all been thinking...

Will Ophelia be able to go on stage tomorrow night?

No-I'm afraid not...

Aurora, who had been sitting with her back to us, suddenly straightened.

What did you say?

It's true, Aurora-it looks like you're on for the Opening after all!

Aggh!!!! <u>Me</u> in front of the PRESS! And Ophelia said Joe Fitt might be there... and Amelie Rose—

Now, now, Aurora - you don't hate anyone. You've just had some unexpected news and it's got you all jittery. What you need now is to rest your voice! The more you shout, the huskier it's getting. So I'm going to order you a nice hot drink, and you can take it up to your room.
And there's no need to worry about your lines tonight - because tomorrow I've called an extra dress rehearsal.
You see! You don't trust I'll be good enough. I bet you want me to go over that STUPID SCENE again. 'Quietly Hysterical!' You can't do—
Aurora - are you MAD? You've just been told you've got the part, and instead of being over the moon... Honestly, if it was me—
You wouldn't understand, Felix - you're just too thick-skinned to be affected by his comments-
Come along now, Aurora - this has gone on long enough. Let's go and find Donna.

me– happily dreaming– ~~vagel~~ ~~vaigl~~ vaguely aware of an unpleasant (yet familiar) sound in my left ear.

I ~~corshu~~ cautiously opened my eyes and saw this — looming down on me–so I shut them again <u>QUICKLY</u>!

Oh, for Heaven's Sake, Hyppolita – **FOCUS!**

Then she rudely dragged me into a sitting position, gripping my face in both her hands.

Now do I have your attention?

You do...

104

What?

Oh Hyppolita — do I have to spell it out?

YES! I have **no** idea what you're talking about!

Right then — Octavia crippled herself and has a nose like a purple balloon —

Yes, Mother, I was there when Ophelia —

And... the **other** one... has lost her voice.

Aurora? She can't have! Her voice is loud enough to fill an airport.

Not today, I gather... Today she can't even raise a squeak.

I suddenly remembered Nigel's warnings last night. I tried not to see the funny side... and failed.

Hee Hee Hee!

So that's why I'm asking how well you know the play.

sudden failure to see funny side as realization begins to dawn.

How well I know the... **Mum!** Mum? Surely you're not - you can't be... **NO WAY!**

I'm **sure** you could do it, Pollypop! It's not such a big part... You're not **totally** stupid, and you must have picked up some **shred** of talent from me somewhere along the line.

She knows how to build a girl's confidence.

You must be joking!

said from deep inside duvet

Oh come on, Polly-Poodle - the show can't go on without you!

ABSOLUTELY <u>NO</u> WAY!

About an hour later I was crouching behind a plywood tree on a San Francisco stage, wearing a baggy old costume, wondering...

How did I let this happen?

and more urgently...

Aggh! What's my next line?

I can't say the dress rehearsal went well...

... So the afternoon was spent going over my scenes one by one with the ~~fellivant~~ relevant actors, who ~~valient~~ valiantly tried not to mention that they'd all had to cancel their massage bookings at the health club.

At 5 o'clock Nigel clapped his hands.

OK-darlings- I think that's about as much as we can do now. Go enjoy the sunshine, get something to eat and relax!

Relax? Yeah right!
I had to go on stage in 2½ hours in front of 900 people!

Could a nightmare get much worse?
Yes...

Polly - What a **TOTAL** DISASTER...

← me trying not to look like I'm going to cry.

That ... **DRESS**!!! It's **DREADFUL**! **Way** too **BIG**! But fear not! Janie from wardrobe will be here in just a mo- to wave her wand.

So I hadn't got the sack!

... Which meant I still had to go on tonight!

Oh and, Polly-

He was still here-

Things then went from bad to worse. Janie
from wardrobe got me to climb onto a
table, and stand there like a dummy
— a very very red dummy —
for about 100 years, while
she pinned the dress.

Right — I'll
have it done by
six — so run
along now, kids,
and have fun!

<u>FUN</u> ? ? ? ! ! !

When I was due on stage in a couple of hours?

Fun was definitely <u>not</u> an option.
Had she said —

Go off and sit in front of a burger
and try not to puke

— I could have done that.

In fact I did do that...
for approximately
one hour.

Then back to the theatre for...

Costume (feeling sick)...

Make-up (feeling sicker)...

Wig (sicker still)...

And suddenly
there I was
in the wings,
peeping
out at this
MASSIVE
audience,
waiting for my
first cue...

<u>AGGH</u>!

I can't say for sure if I said my lines at the right time
we'd got to the very last scene.

or in the right place, but in what felt like seconds

By Polly Price

And then it was all over, and I was being hauled on
stage for the curtain call.

I'd got through it and... I'd quite enjoyed it!
There were even a couple of moments when I
almost believed I was Sarah and that I had a
brother, and we were on the run!

But just when I thought it was finally over, they all
started talking about getting ready for the party.

NO WAY was I going to that.

I've been to too many Opening Night parties—standing
around in dark corners while actors go:

Daahling-you were Sensational!

Simply marvellous, Luvvy! ...to my mum.

So I sneaked back to the dressing room, got my jeans on and headed for the door.

> Where do you think you're off to, Sweetie?

BUM. Nigel was blocking my exit, ~~brandesh~~ brandishing a huge carrier bag.

> I sent Donna off this afternoon to pick you out something for the party - just in case it slipped your mind. So — see you there!

And off he skipped - leaving me with a big bag, an open mouth and this ↓

Orlando

THE COLISEUM
PARKWAY DRIVE. SAN FRANCISCO

welcomes

------ Polly Price ------

to

Torn Asunder

Opening party
Friday 27th July
10 pm onwards

I looked in the bag. Inside was one of those shimmering dresses I'd fallen for in Orlando's. There was even a matching pair of satin ballet pumps in my size!

Janie from wardrobe helped to make me ~~unfekon~~ ~~unfeckoni~~ unrecognizable and then took this picture → to prove it!

Before I could change my mind we were all whooshed off to The ~~Colesium~~ Coliseum, and into a sea of flashing cameras.

I just concentrated on getting through them all without tripping over, and I'd finally made it into the {Banqueting Suite} when Will nudged me and pointed.

Ophelia and Aurora were looking straight at us — without any obvious sign of affection.

To be honest I was a bit surprised to see them.

Do you think they watched the show?

Before I could answer we were suddenly surrounded...

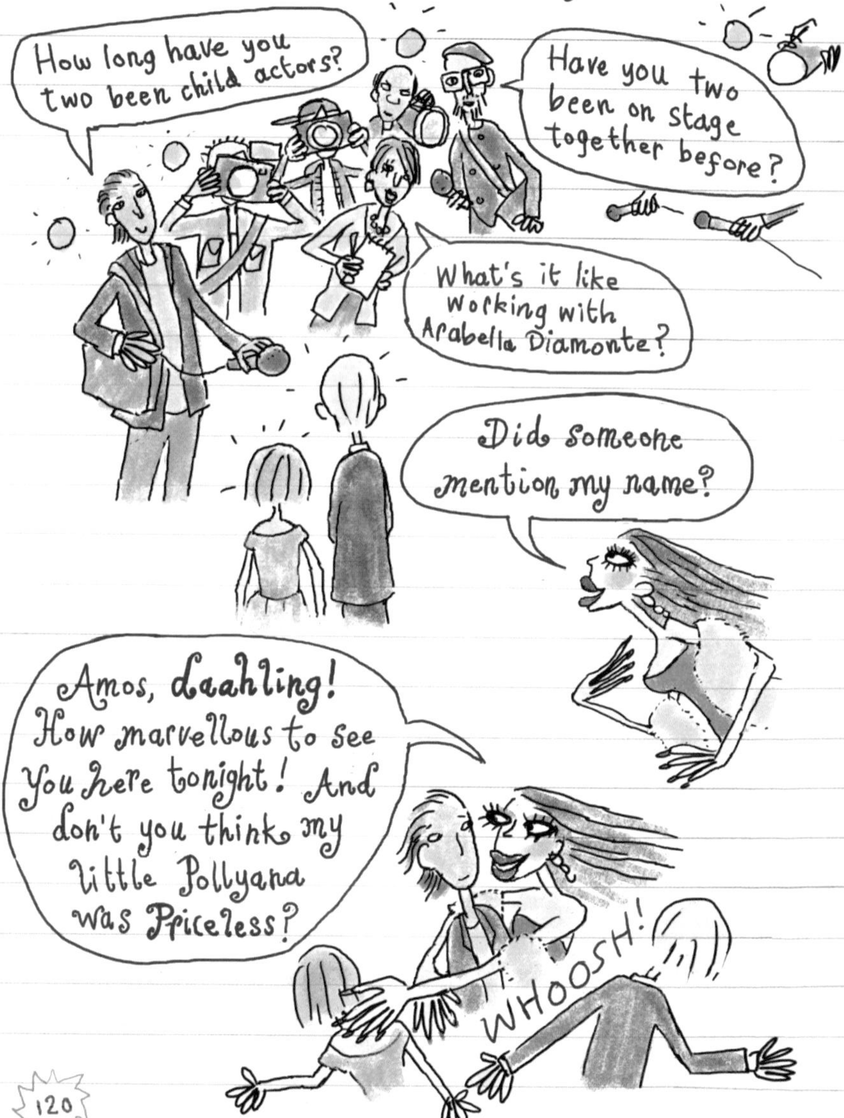

ABOUT AN HOUR LATER

I'm sitting in one of the toilets trying to avoid EVERYONE.

As soon as my mum released me I tried to find Will to say sorry. He was right on the other side of the room, sitting on a huge sofa with Felix, balancing plates of food on their laps. They totally looked like they didn't want to be ~~interupt~~ interrupted, so I just stayed where I was, remembering how much I hate Opening nights.

But a few seconds later, standing by yourself feeling lonely seemed like a really cosy option — because Ophelia and Aurora were heading straight for me... and something told me they weren't coming over to say...

You were marvellous, darling

Fortunately crutches slow you down. Even more fortunately ballet shoes don't.

I had already spotted the Ladies sign →

(an old and highly useful escape strategy)

So I ~~herted~~ hurtled straight for it.

TROUBLE is I've now totally caught up with everything that's happened and I'm COMPLETELY STARVING.

Ophelia and Aurora **must** have gone by now.

I suppose I have to leave here sometime.

Might as well be now.

ME

~~ignominiously~~ hiding in the toilets (very posh and shiny with lots of ~~marbel~~ marble everywhere - like a palace!)

checking no one's coming

pen found on floor by sink

lid down!

paper towel (I stupidly left my diary in the ~~swe~~ Banqueting Suite)

This is much harder to write on.

MUCH LATER

I put my head down (this way you can't catch anyone's eye) and charged towards the food table.

A crutch was blocking my way.

quite good imitation of my mother's voice

Where do you think you're going, Polly-Poooo?

quite good imitation of a strangulated mouse

Er...Nowhere...

loud enough to get _everyone_ interested

Not off to find someone else's part to _steal_ then?

squeakier than a strangulated bat

I didn't steal your part, Ophelia.

~~horse~~ hoarse but _loud_ whisper

How did mice, bats and horses get into this?

No, you stole MINE!

Aggh! I've run out of notebook - so I'm adding some paper I borrowed from Will.

You've been planning it all along, haven't you?
Hanging around us, sucking up to the boys,
sneaking about, spying, secretly learning our lines
... until you finally got what you wanted.
Only, I am afraid - <u>Little Miss Thief</u> - you can't
steal **TALENT**! Or good press reviews!
And I'm sure you won't need <u>me</u> to tell you
you were a complete **DISASTER** on stage -
everyone thought so.

me - trying to look like
I'm not going to cry for
the <u>2nd</u> time tonight

Actually - I thought Polly's
Performance was immensely
moving...

Nigel was grinning down at me!
Then suddenly people all around joined in...

I thought so too

She's a fine
little actress!

Utterly
believable

Then one of the reporters said:

> Both the kids were great tonight. How about a shot of the girl and her brother?

And the next thing I knew, Will was being dragged over and they were taking pictures of us both!

I got given this one! →

When they finally finished with us, Will turned to me...

> You'd better come and rescue your plate of food, Poll. I saw Aurora eyeing up your sausage roll just now!

> My plate of food?

> We've been patiently waiting for the **CHILD-STAR** to come and grace us with her presence!

And as I squeezed on the sofa between Will and Felix, stuffing what was left of the sausage roll into my mouth, I suddenly knew that this had to be the end of the **BEST** day ever—

and **NOTHING** could mess that up...

What does she look like in that dress?

A lampshade!

... Absolutely **NOTHING**!!!

Letitia Milton *reviews*
TORN ASUNDER
****

Rondo Theatre

This gruelling, yet touching World War Two drama is beautifully directed by Nigel Dillane, featuring an all-British cast fresh from London's West End.

Daniel Hopkins, as ever, is chillingly powerful in the role of Gestapo Officer Otto Schmidt. And American audiences are treated to the surprising casting of Arabella Diamonte in the role of Elsa, the mother whose life is torn asunder by the horrific events in Germany at the time. Diamonte plays the role with characteristic gusto, which at times seems just a little ebullient in the circumstances.

An unexpected bonus is the debut performance of Hyppolita Price, real-life daughter playing stage daughter, Sarah. She and William Granger (Hugo) were genuinely compelling as brother and sister on the run.

I'd also like to make a special mention of Ron Slimey as the dead officer, who lies remarkably still at the front of the stage for practically twenty minutes.

All in all a great night out!

Arabella Diamonte with her daughter, Hyppolita, last night at the opening of **Torn Asunder.**

I looked this up. It means cheerful and full of energy or boiling and agitated!!!

I wasn't too sure about compelling — it means forcing attention — but everyone says it's a good thing!!

THE RONDO THEATRE
GEARY STREET, SFO.
PRESENTS
TORN ASUNDER
* * * *
JUL 27 7:30PM
N. 56 38.00
ORCH
JUL 27

this is
for swizzling
drinks →

Torn
Asunder

27th July

Thank you Polly.

You were a wonderful

Sarah tonight.

I was so proud! Nigel x